Creative Keyboard Presents

JAZZ STUDIES FOR PIANO

MW00450665

by Paul T. Smith

CONTENTS

Creative Keyboard Publications MEL BAY

Visit us on the Web at www.melbay.com — E-mail us at email@melbay.com

CHECK OUT CREATIVE KEYBOARD'S *FREE WEBZINE* @ www.creativekeyboard.com

CONTENTS

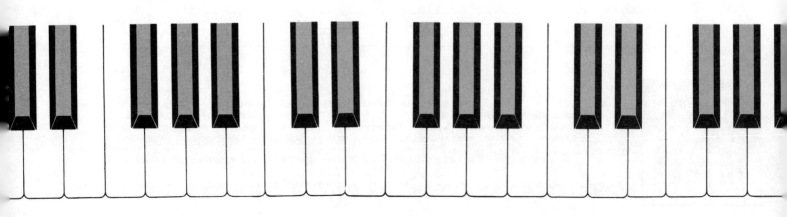

PAUL T. SMITH

Pianist Extraordinaire

Dominic Mumolo Photography

In America, jazz critics agree, Paul Smith is jazz piano. In Europe the *Jazz Dictionary* says "Paul Smith is the greatest pianist from America." Now celebrating 60 years in the music industry, Paul is extremely well known throughout the field of music as a "World Class Pianist." His command of the keyboard is awesome!

Paul's credits include Pianist/Arranger for the Tommy Dorsey Orchestra, Staff Pianist at Warner Brothers Studios, Staff Pianist at NBC Studios for over 12 years, and Pianist/Arranger for Pat Boone during the 1960s. He was the Arranger/Pianist/Conductor on Bing Crosby's last two albums, *Southern Memoirs* and *Bingo Viejo*.

His TV credits include Pianist/Arranger for the following shows; Red Skelton, Dinah Shore, Nat King Cole, Bing Crosby, Carol Burnett, Jo Stafford, Gordon McCrae, Tony Martin and many more.

For two years he was Pianist/Conductor for the Steve Allen TV Show, Pianist for four years for Sammy Davis Jr., and 11 years as Pianist/Conductor for Ella Fitzgerald.

Paul has just completed three years of Community Concerts for Columbia Artists, and currently doing concerts with duo and trio. He also plays for a new show, *Hollywood's Secret Singing Stars*. Among his many notable appearances, Paul recently starred at **Carnegie Hall** and Alice Tully hall in the **Lincoln Center**, New York, **Symphony Hall** in Boston, **Kennedy Center** in Washington, D.C. **Resorts International** in Atlantic City, the **Dorothy Chandler Pavilion** and **Hollywood Bowl** in Los Angeles, **Fairmont Hotels** in San Francisco, New Orleans and Dallas, the **Sands, Caesar's Palace, Sahara, Flamingo, Desert Inn**, and **Fremont** hotels in Las Vegas, and **Prince Albert Hall** in London, England. He has made numerous appearances at major locations throughout Asia. He often stars in jazz festivals in Denver, Midland, Sarasota, Scottsdale, San Diego and Irvine.

Paul is the star on over 50 albums for such labels as Capitol, M-G-M, Verve, Warner Brothers, Discovery and several others. He has many albums, tapes and CDs available on Outstanding Records. He has recorded and played for top talent including Pearl Bailey, Rosemary Clooney, Edie Adams, Billy May, Marty Paich, Ray Anthony, Alfred Newman, Joni James, Toni Tennille, Mel Torme, John Green and Paul Weston.

His records are often played on radio stations throughout the world, including the BBC, Voice of America, etc., and in particular they are featured on KLON-FM, America's #1 jazz radio station in Long Beach, California. Via the Playboy satellite system, it reaches all the nations of North and South America and the Pacific Rim.

EXERCISES FOR THE CONTEMPORARY PIANIST

This is an unusual exercise book. You will find no fingering marking on most of the exercises. This is because you are to finger them in whatever way is comfortable for you. If you wish to use your thumb for 5 notes in succession, it's OK. As long as it gets the job done.

The exercises are technically demanding and are written in all keys, rather than just in C. Most of them are figures which may be incorporated into solos that you will play when you improvise.

These exercises are not meant to replace the Hanon and Czerny exercises which have been the basis for a solid technique throughout the years. Rather this is to supplement those exercises by moving into a more modern and progressive group of studies which are not found in the older exercises.

These exercises are meant to be more fun to play—more challenging in a modern way and to give the student a chance to invent his or her own fingering for the exercises.

A lot of the exercises are jazz-oriented and jazz-players will find a lot of them are practical for use in improvisional situations. By putting accents where the student feels they should be, the exercises become jazz figures in certain instances.

The exercises are written with the idea of getting away from the constant scale patterns of typical technique exercises. You will find a few that remind you of Hanon, however the majority of them are designed to be musically enjoyable as well as technically demanding. Some of them will stretch your hands a little beyond what you are used to doing in that area.

Having a proficient left hand is something that should be worked on diligently and the suggested way to play the two-handed exercises is to play the left hand much louder than the right. Usually the left hand just "goes along for the ride" and the right hand plays aggressively and the left hand follows. I like to reverse that procedure by accenting the left hand and letting the right hand follow along, for a change. It's also a very interesting procedure to just let the right hand "pretend to play" while the left hand is digging in. In other words, just touch the keys with the right hand so it seems to be playing the figures while the left hand is actually accentuating the figures.

I'll have a brief comment on each exercise as you go through the book and I'm sure you'll enjoy playing this collection of modern exercises.

ALL EXERCISES ARE TO BE PLAYED WITH A METRONOME.

Paul T. Smith

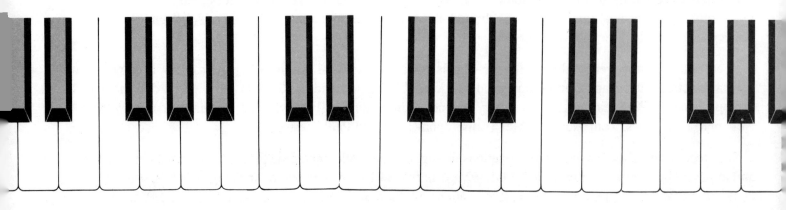

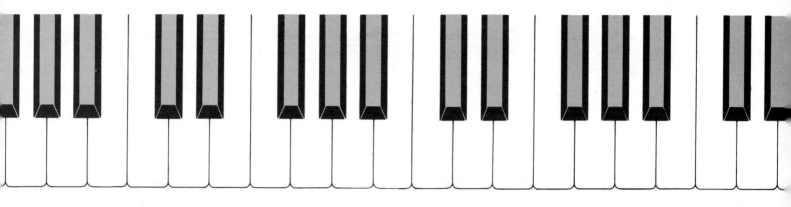

The interval exercises are the first examples of "find your own fingering".

Most of the fingering is obvious—there are usually only one or two ways that it is practical to finger most exercises so just find the most comfortable one and go ahead and do it.

INTERVAL EXERCISES

USING THE EXERCISE

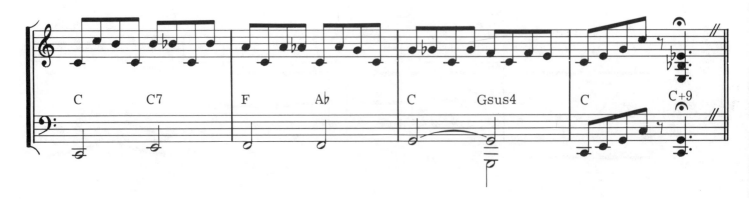

INTERVAL EXERCISES (CON.)

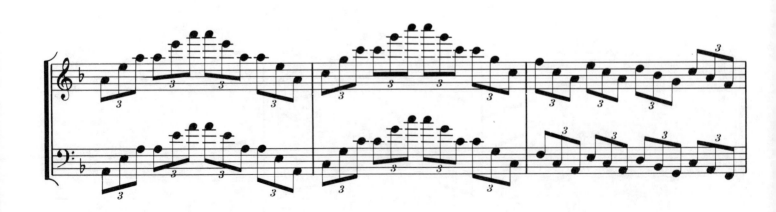

11

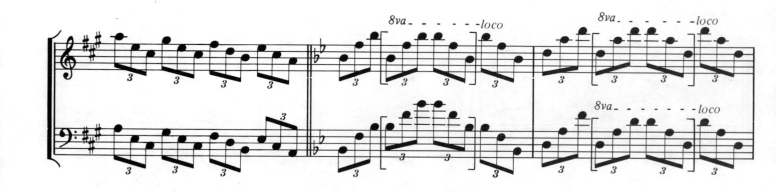

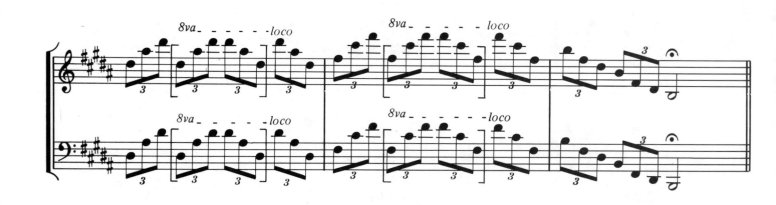

USING THE EXERCISE

INTERVAL EXERCISES (CON.)

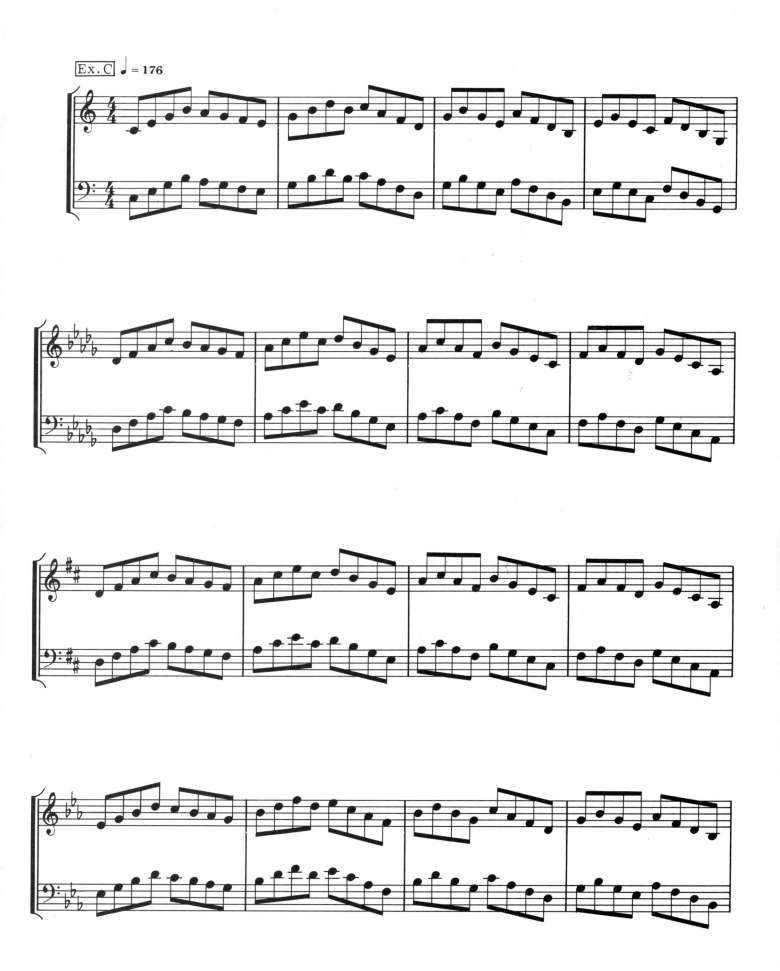

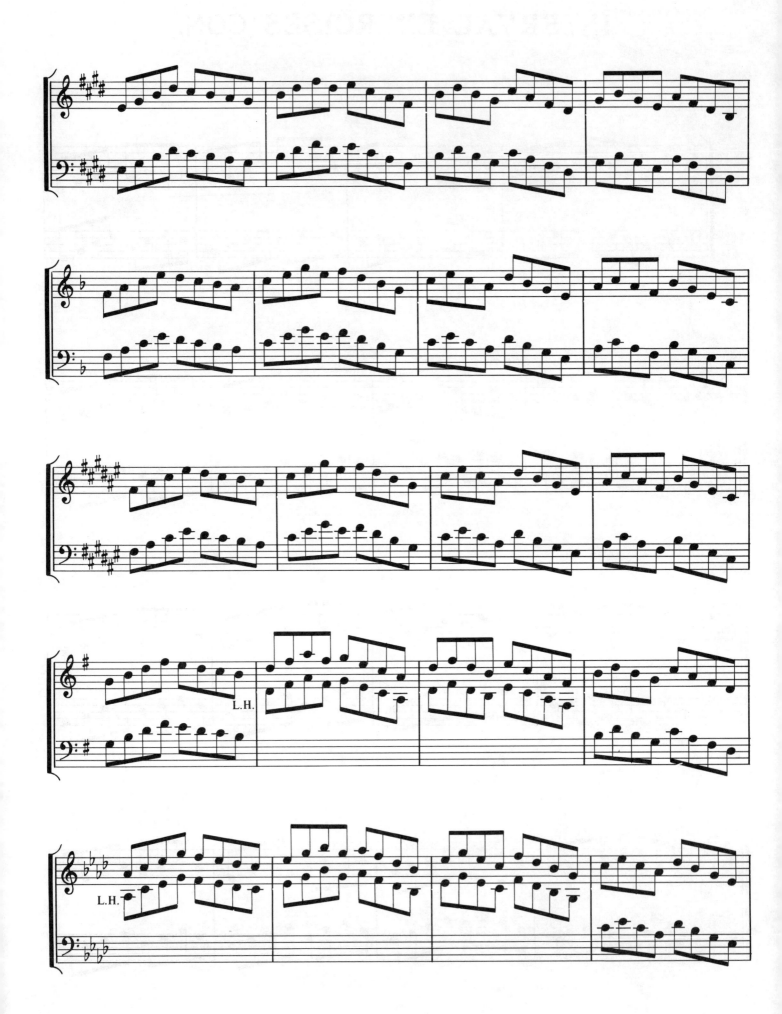

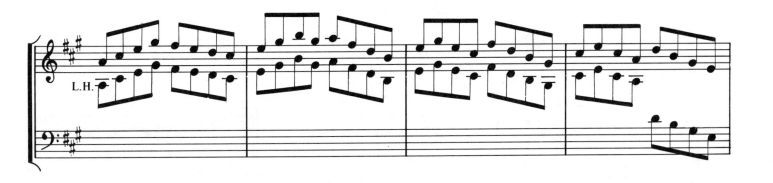

USING THE EXERCISE

16

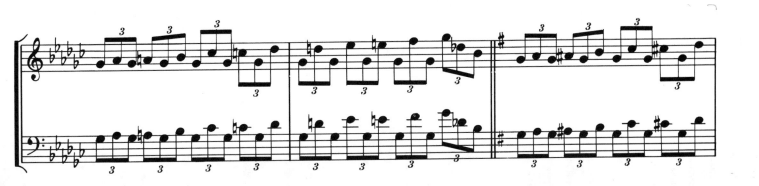

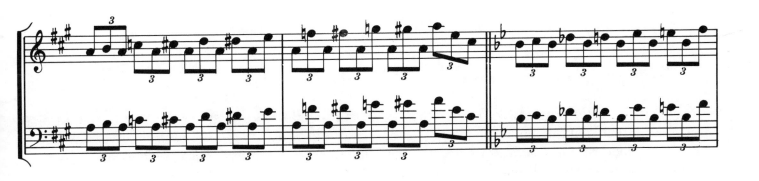

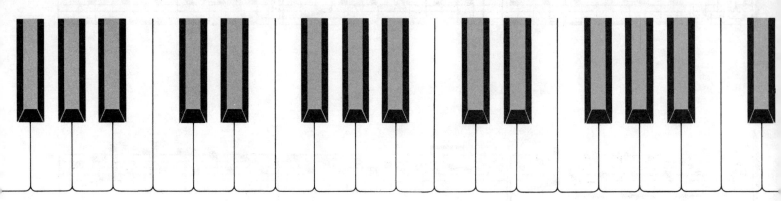

This is a little progressive figure which is written in all the keys and needs you to put a few accents in to give it the modern feeling. I haven't marked any accents so it is entirely up to how you feel it. A good rule-of-thumb is to increase your volume as you go up the scale—it seems to swing better that way. The left hand just holds steady and the passing tones are legato.

JAZZ EXERCISE FOR RIGHT HAND

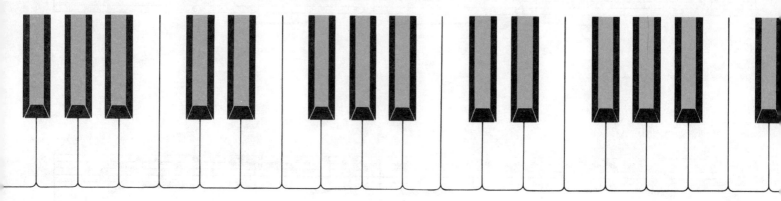

This is a more standard-type of exercise which encompasses all the keys and the same fingering is to be used in all the keys. The exercise starts with the 5th finger in the right hand and the thumb in the left and stays that way throughout the entire exercise. No deviation from the basic fingering pattern.

8 BAR TWO-HANDED EX. IN ALL KEYS

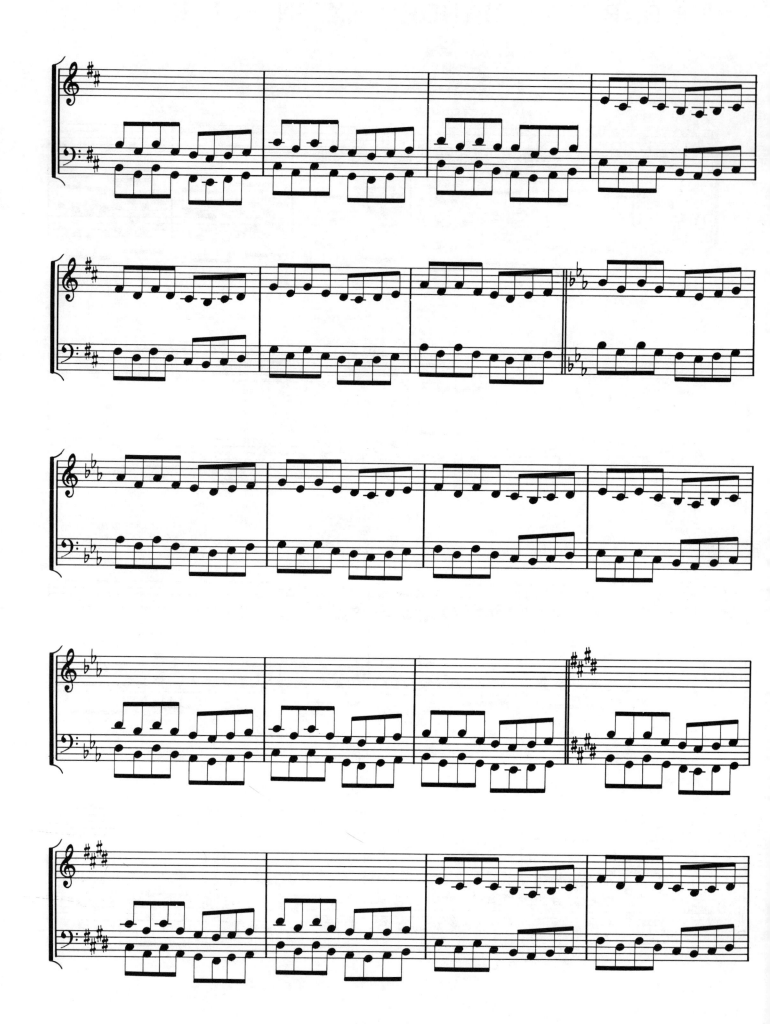

24

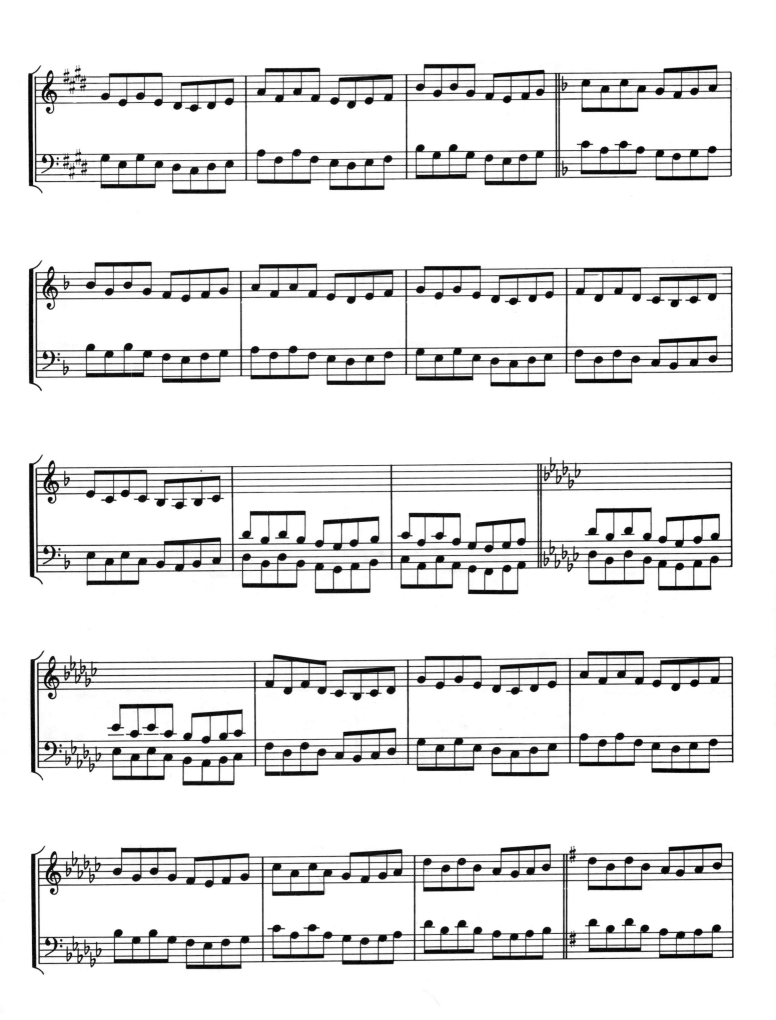

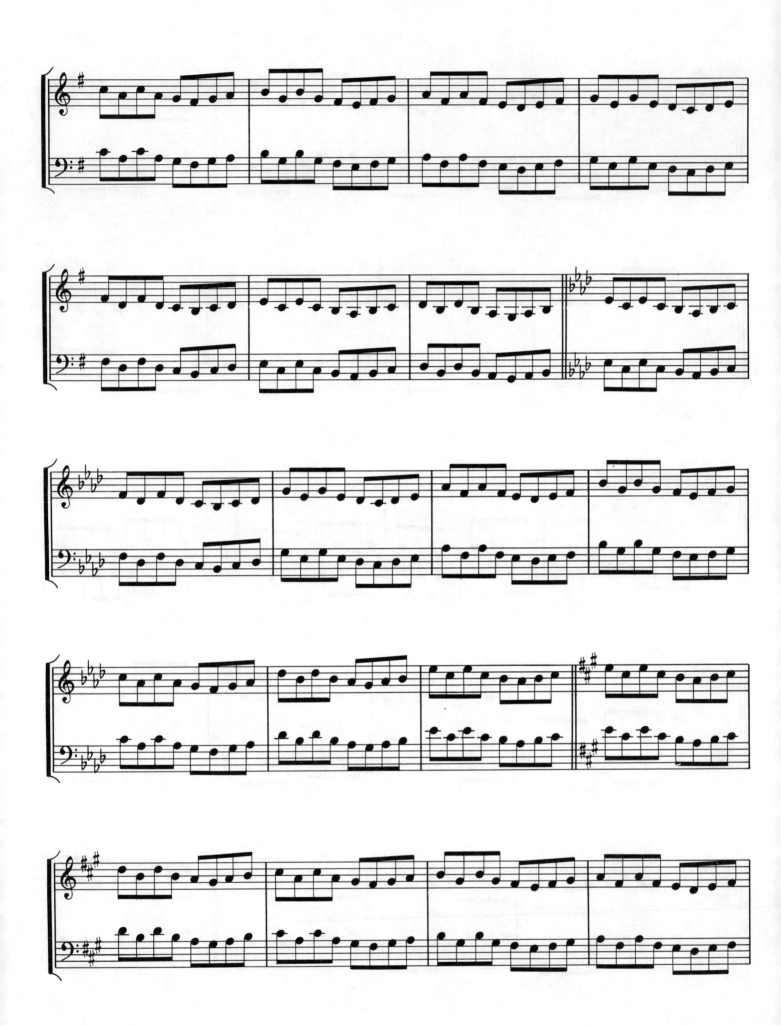

27

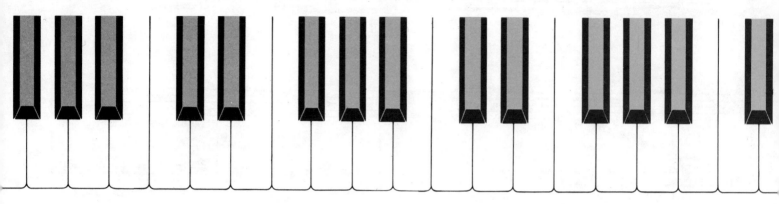

This could be called an exercise in 3rds. It's based on the chord progression of a very well-known standard. See if you can guess what the basic song is. It's especially effective if you can get it up to a roaring tempo.

MELODIC EXERCISE

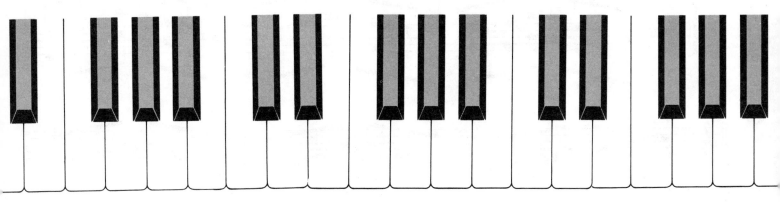

These arpeggios briefly go through the major, minor, augmented and diminished phases. Find a fingering that is comfortable for you and proceed. You may find that is convenient to play the 4th and 5th notes of each measure with the same fingers. 5–5 in the right hand and 1–1 in the left. That eliminates any awkward hand positions in trying to finger it in some "legitimate" way. Right hand runs 1–2–3–5–5–3–2–1. Left hand runs 5–3–2–1–1–2–3–5 etc.

ALL-KEY ARPEGGIOS

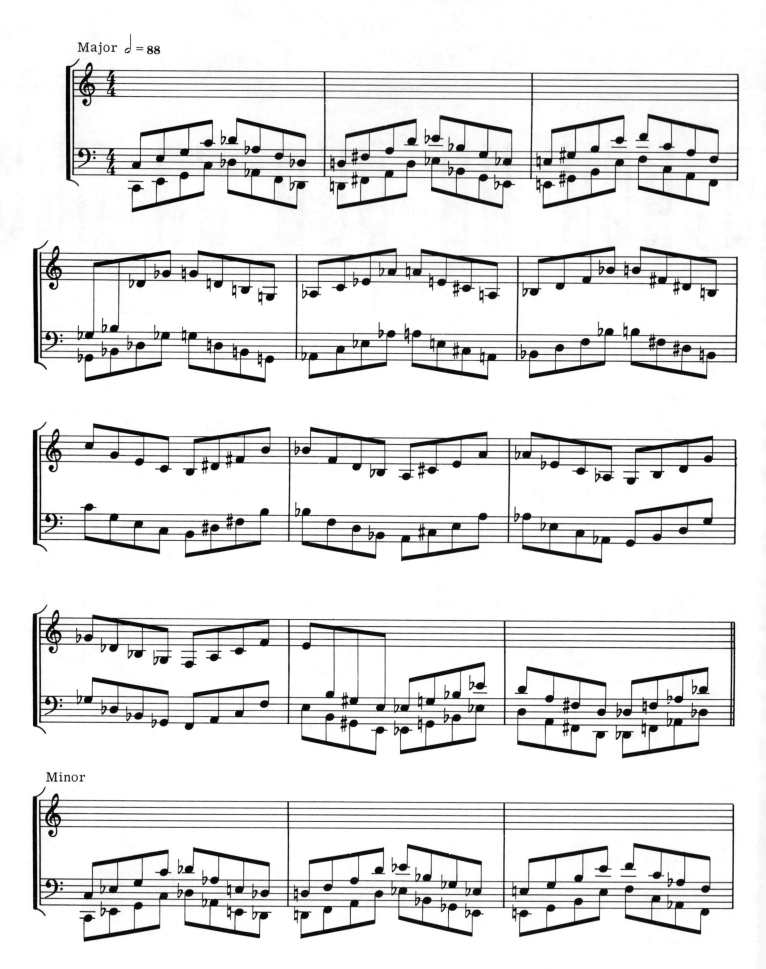

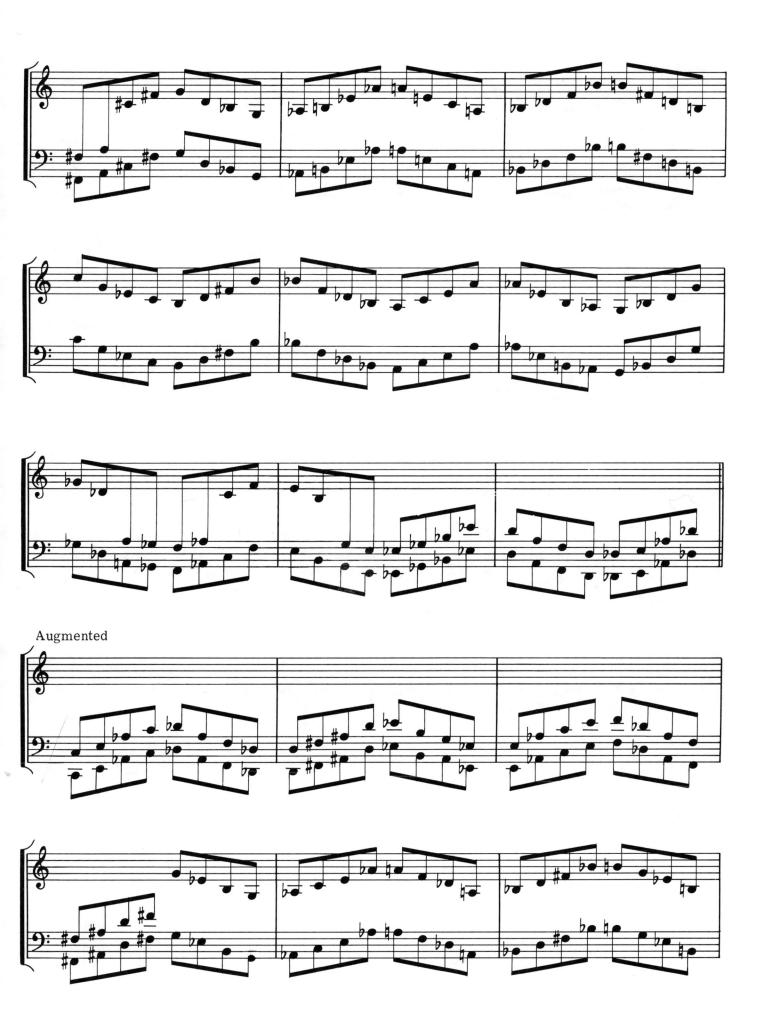

Augmented

33

Diminished

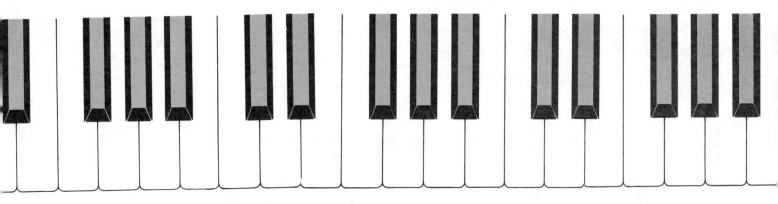

Here you have a series of conventional scales and your only problem is how to finger them. You'll have to change, according to the black and white keys. Get used to reading the exercises and not trying to memorize them so you can watch your hands. The less you watch your hands, the better pianist you will be.

SCALES GALONE

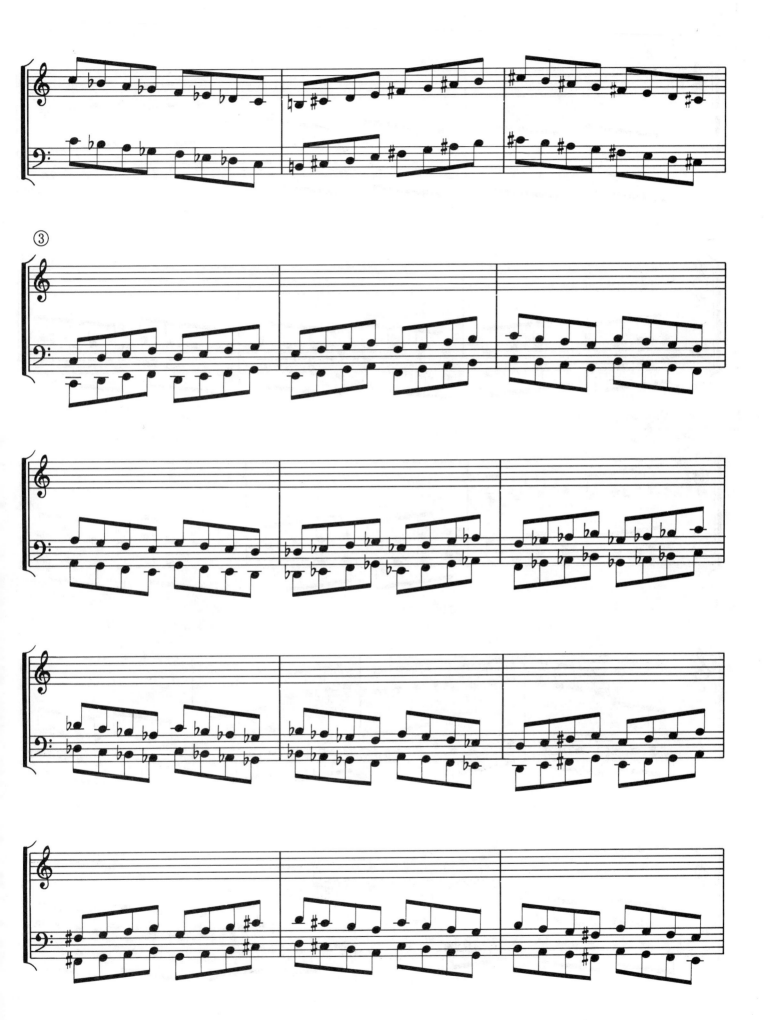

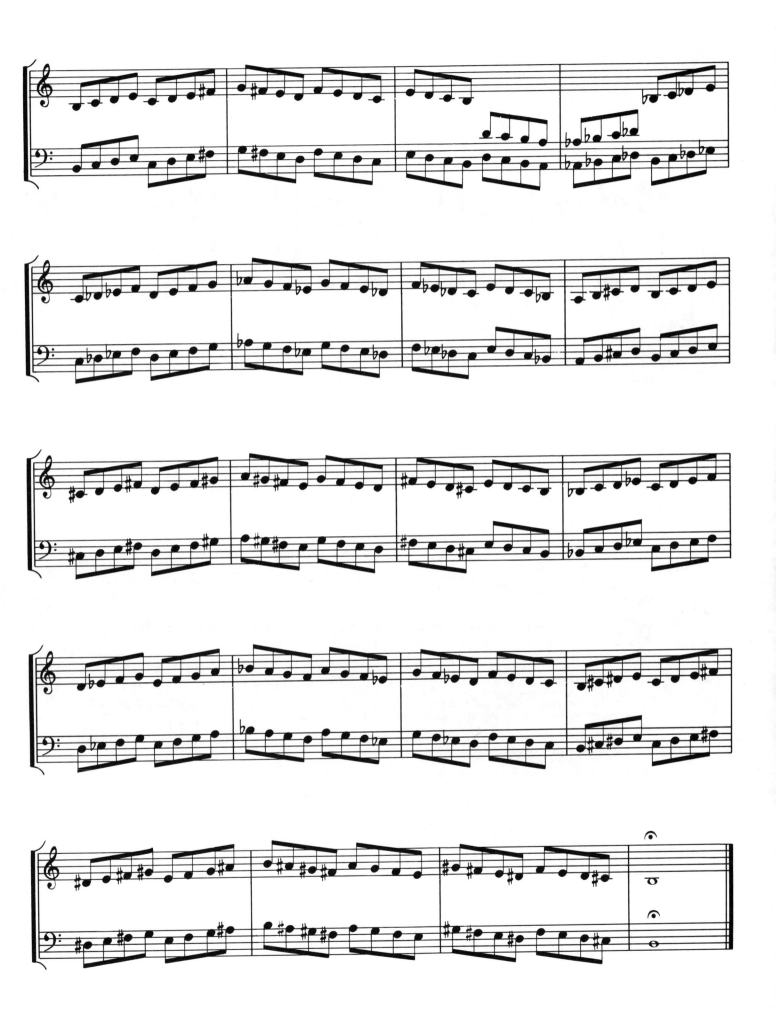

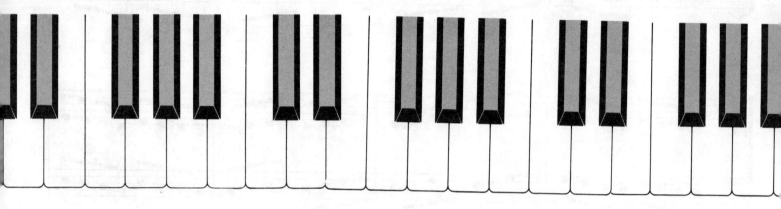

This can be an exciting piece to play if you can get it up to an extremely fast tempo. Naturally you practice it slowly at first, then increase your tempo gradually.

There are two fingerings which may be used. One is to use 3 and 2 on the right hand notes in the 1st 3 measures of each key. The other, which will slow you down a little, is to use 1–1, then 2–2, 1–1, 3–3, 1–1, 4–4, 1–1, 5–5, etc with 5–5 continuing up to where the triplet arpeggio starts.

The left hand note can be played with either 1–2 or 3, depending on which is best for you. I prefer 2 myself, which is the happy medium and kind of keeps the left hand out of the way of the right. You decide which is right for you.

DOUBLE NOTE EX. A

43

45

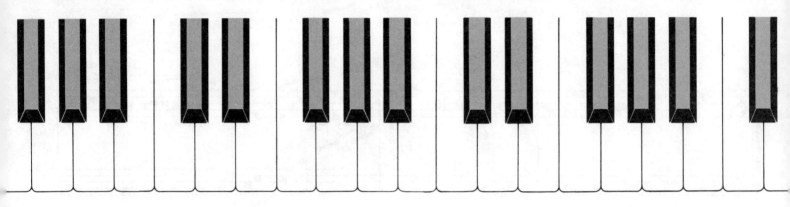

In this exercise, the left hand note is played with the 3rd finger all the way. The right hand single notes are all played with the thumb and the thirds are played in whatever progression of fingers is easiest for you. They can be played with the same two fingers wherever it is convenient so you don't have to figure out a complicated system of fingering them. The exercise is to be played in a staccato manner so the thirds don't have to be fingered in order (1–3, 2–4, 3–5 etc). Possibly 4–2, 4–2, 4–2 etc. Again, it is up to your own discretion as to how you play the thirds. Make it easy on yourself.

DOUBLE NOTE EX. B

Ped.

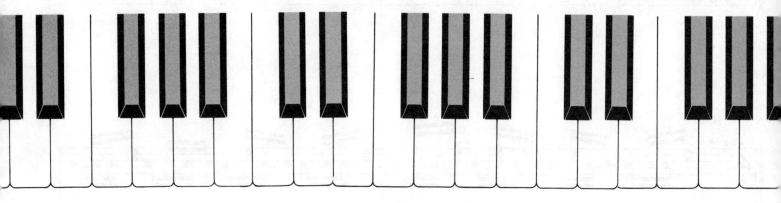

This is a little lilting jazz waltz exercise which will give you a little exercise in stretching the hand to play 4ths. The hand should be in position over the notes to be played at all times. In the key of C, the logical fingering is 5–2 to 3–1. In D flat, it's 4–2 to 3–1 etc. The key determines the fingering, naturally. Just make sure you don't develop any awkward hand movements during this exercise.

4THS FOR RIGHT HAND

Key of C

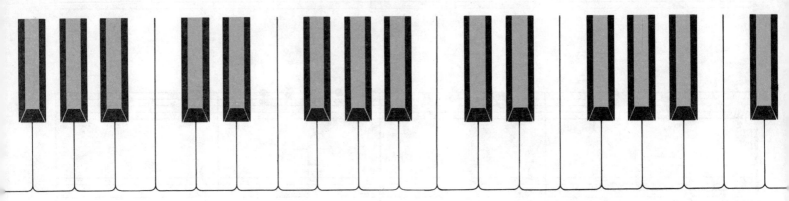

Rather than write out the entire exercise in octaves, I have just written the one octave notes and you may add the octave above in the right hand and below in the left. Play it as legato as possible, keeping the hands close to the keyboard. Occasionally you may want to use 4–1 instead of 5–1 when moving from black to white or white to black. This gives you a more legato sound than playing all octaves 5–1. You can use a little pedal in this exercise to avoid the staccato effect of the octaves. Remember, the more legato, the better.

OCTAVE EXERCISES

58

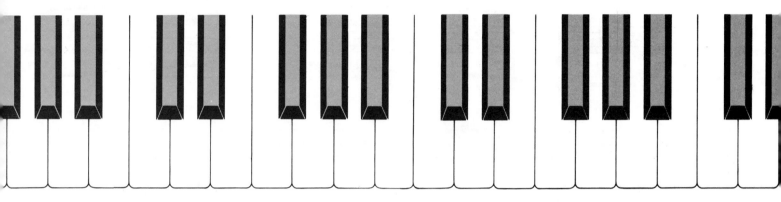

After having written this exercise, I discovered that it was a rather difficult one to play. It's meant to exercise the 3rd and 4th fingers and, instead of resorting to our usual strong 1st and 2nd fingers, we play these exercises with 3 and 4. It's especially difficult in negotiating the black and white keys with these two fingers.

EXERCISE FOR 4-3 AND 3-4

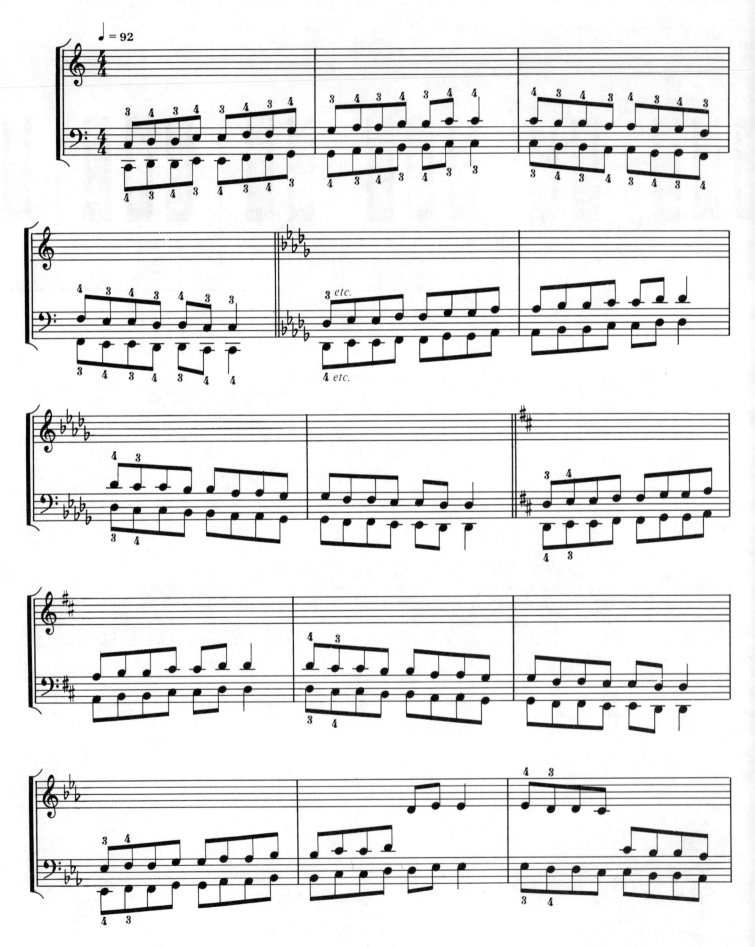

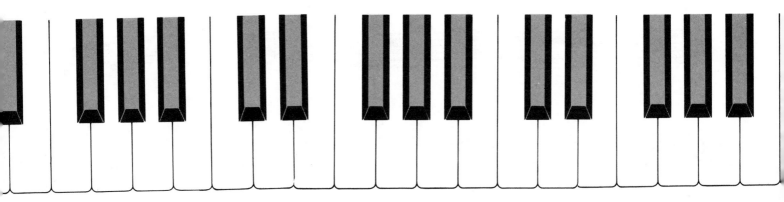

After having struggled through the preceding 3–4, 4–3, exercise, this left-hand exercise should be no puzzler at all. This is a straight-ahead scale-type exercise in all keys with the right hand just holding it together harmonically. Play it relaxed and smoothly and articulate the left hand.

PUZZLER FOR LEFT HAND

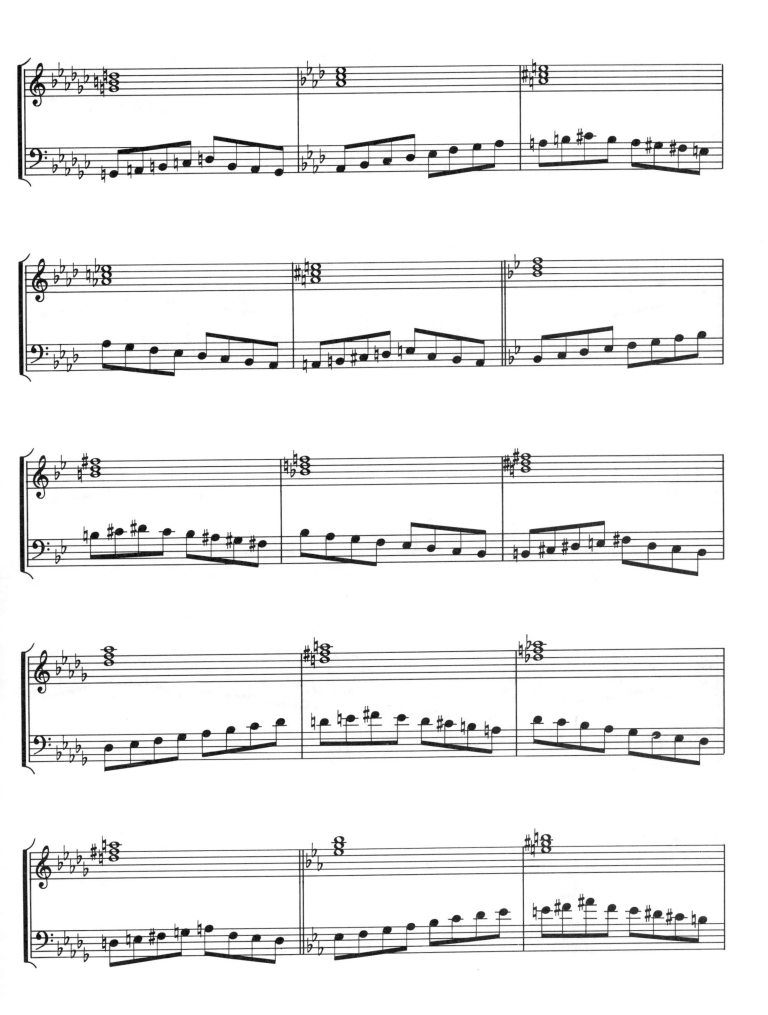

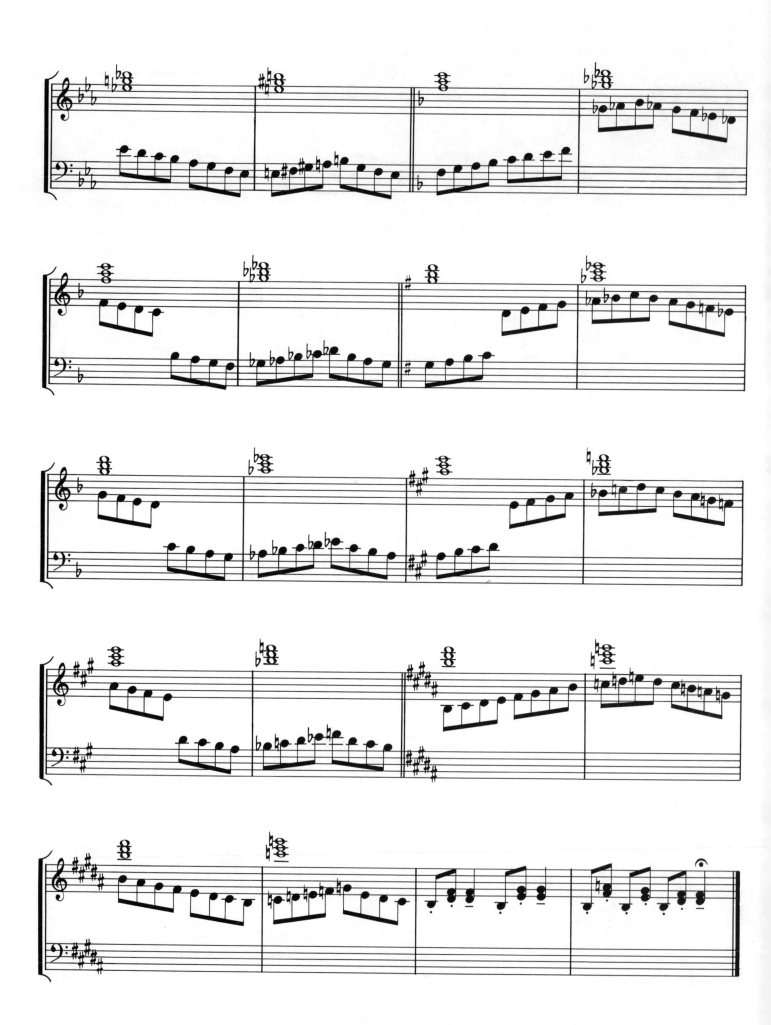

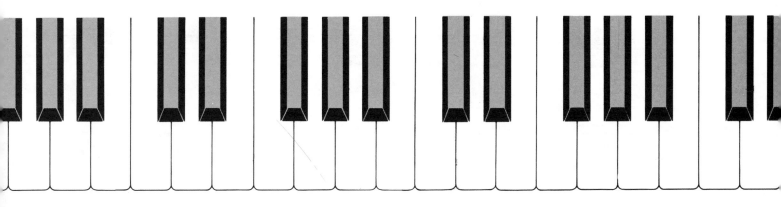

This is a simple exercise, once you get the **idea** of bouncing the hands off one another. It is to be played in a staccato manner, very clean and well-articulated. This type of figure is also very effective as a rhythmic background to another soloist. In jazz we call it "comping".

The left hand must be as strong as the right hand on this exercise and no pedal is to be used. Strictly staccato all the way.

CO-ORDINATION EXERCISE A

71

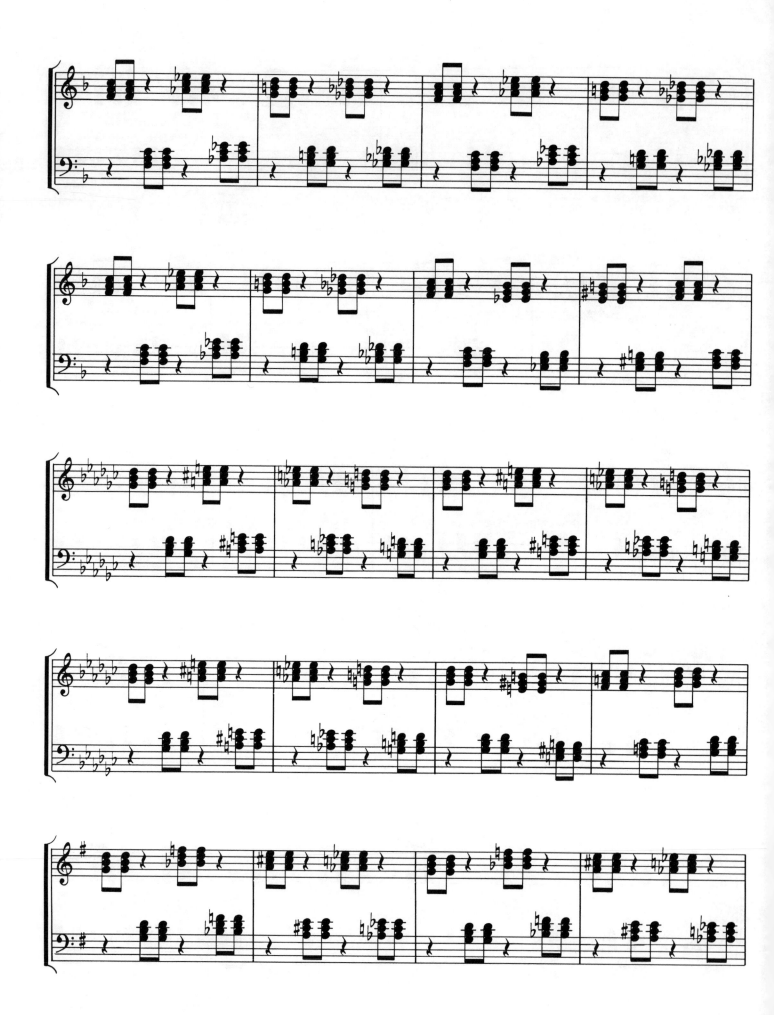

72

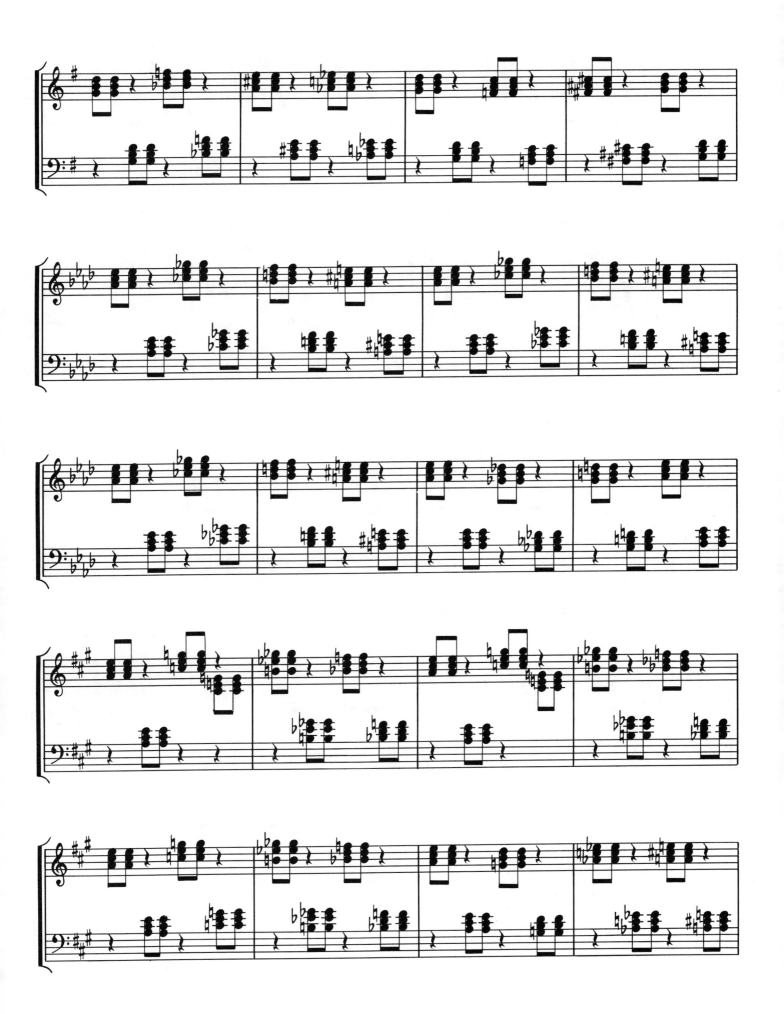

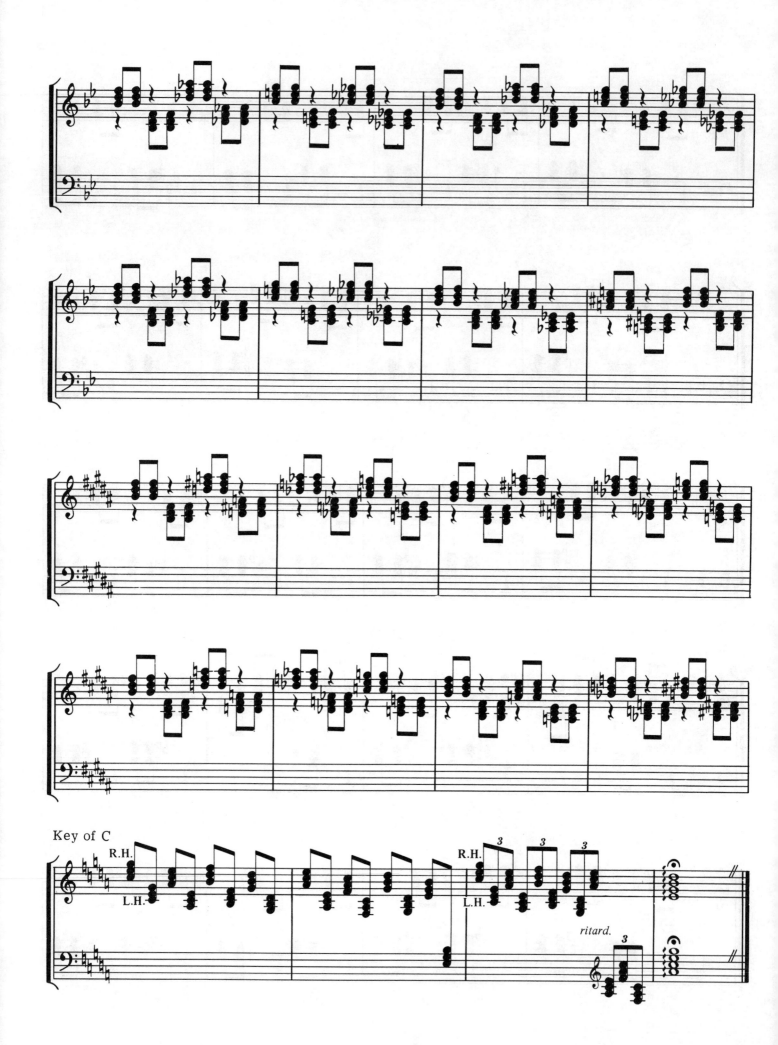

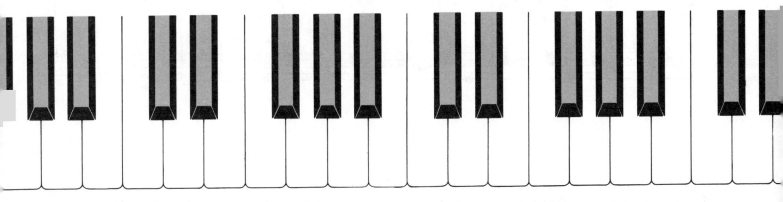

The thing to be avoided on this little exercise is the feeling that the left hand is starting on the downbeat. After you have this exercise mastered, try accenting the left hand and see if it throws you off time-wise. Simply put, the right-hand figure is basically just two sets of quarter triplets with the left hand stuck in between each note of the quarter triplet, thus making it a series of 8th triplets. The metronome is a MUST on this exercise so you will always know where ONE is.

CO-ORDINATION EXERCISE B

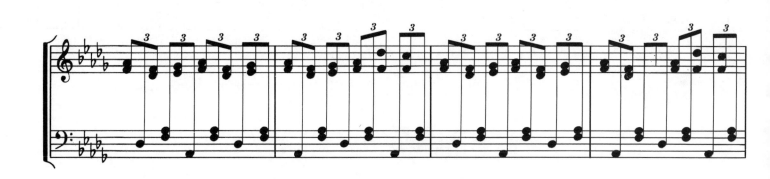

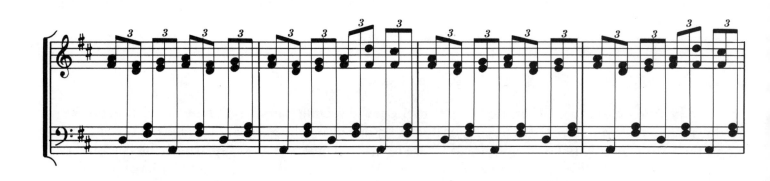

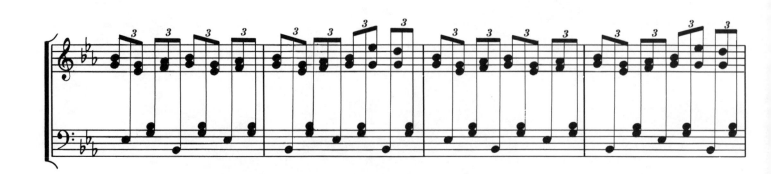

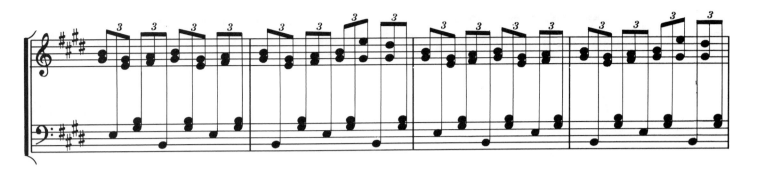

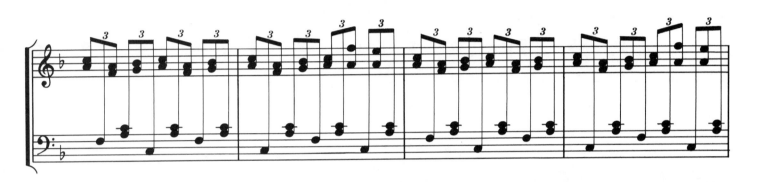

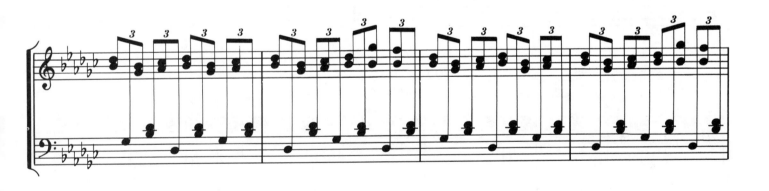

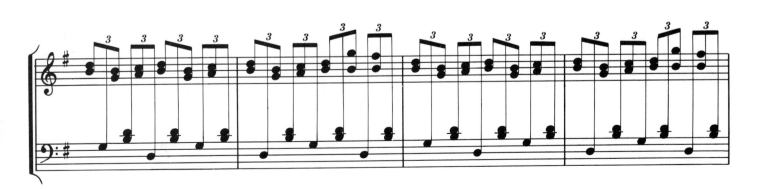

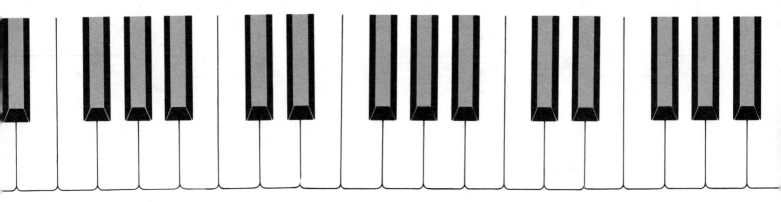

This is a little 5/4 rhythm exercise which is meant only to get you acquainted with the 5 beats to a bar for a while. The figure is the stock rhythm of the 5/4 beat and is used in most pieces written in that time.

5/4 EXERCISE

82

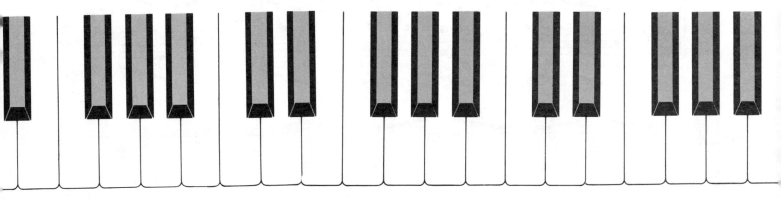

The title may be a little misleading since there is only one note in each hand, however they are an octave apart so it's partly an octave exercise. This is another case of using two notes played by one finger. This exercise is similar to interval Ex. B except that it is done in one octave sections and goes up chromatically.

The 3rd and 4th notes of each measure may be played by the same finger if it is convenient for you to do so.

CHROMATIC OCTAVE EX.

Key of G

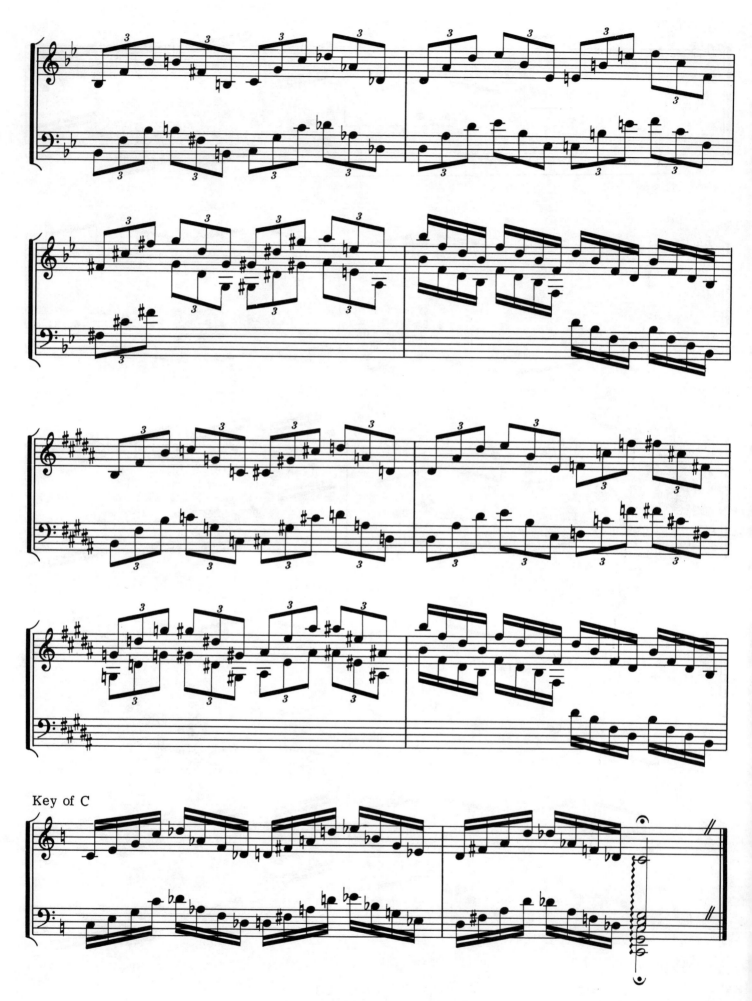

Key of C

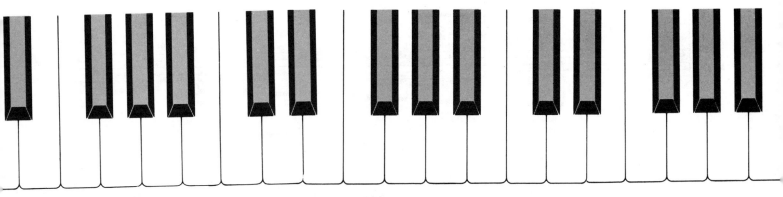

This is a rising scale exercise done in a slightly different way. In coming down at the 4th measure of each exercise, you will have to play the arpeggios 5–3–2–1, then 5–3–2–1 again in the right hand. 1–2–3–5, then 1–2–3–5 in the left hand. Then start the next progression on the same finger that you just used.

A SLIGHTLY DIFFICULT EXERCISE

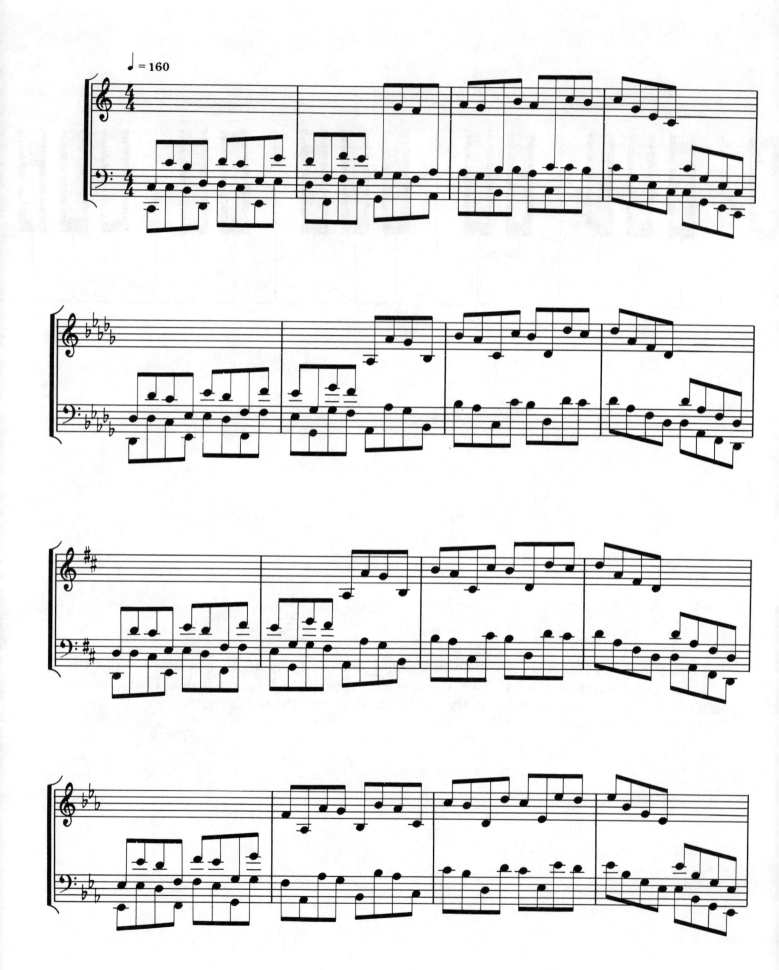

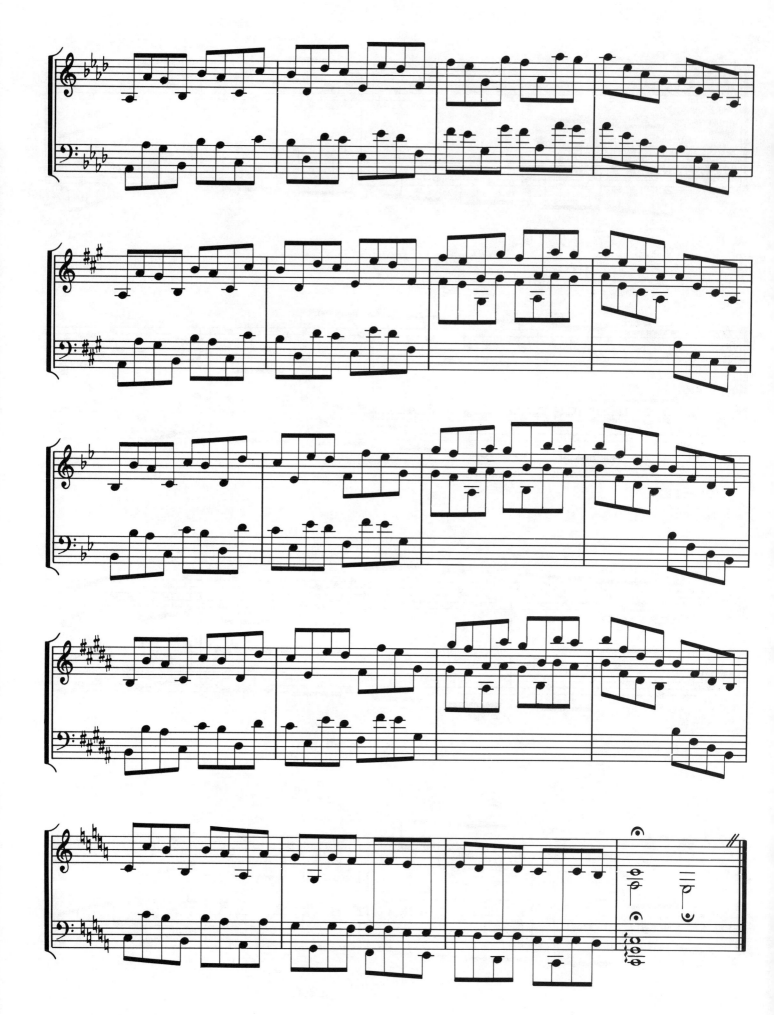

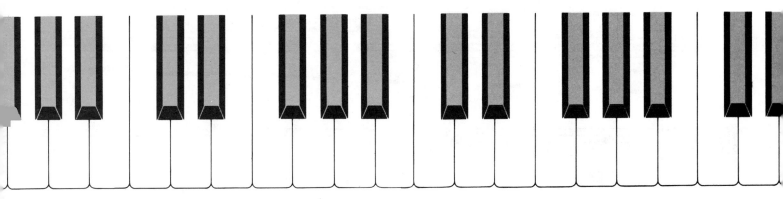

The main difficulty with this exercise is reading all the sharps, flats and naturals. Make sure you are aware of what key you are playing in at all times. It isn't as hard as it may look but you have to be on top of your reading at all times. Especially watch the progression of triplets at the end of each phrase.

Make the fingering as simple as you can—you may be able to finger each key in a similar manner but the sharp keys will cause you to change that idea.

A MORE DIFFICULT EXERCISE

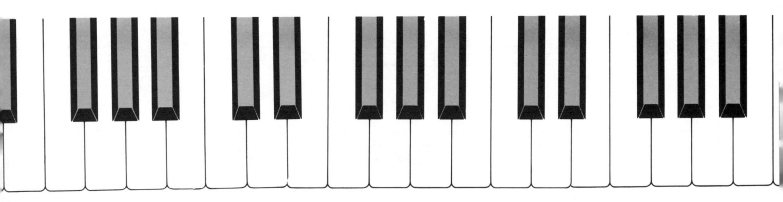

The only reason for the title is that it has no connection with anything else in this book. It is a jazz-oriented piece with some technical stumbling blocks. Watch your D.S. and Coda signs.

Especially use the metronome on this one since there are many places where you will have the tendency to go fast cause the figures are easy and slow down where some of the figures become more difficult.

Always set your metronome at the speed that makes it possible for you to play the hard parts at that particular speed.

I hope this whole series of exercises has been a help to you in improving your technical abilities.

Paul T. Smith

THE SILLY EXERCISE

OTHER BOOKS BY THE AUTHOR

JAZZ STUDIES FOR PIANO

JAZZ SOLOS FOR PIANO

JAZZ BALLADS

JAZZ/ROCK SOLOS

BLUES/BOOGIE SOLOS FOR PIANO

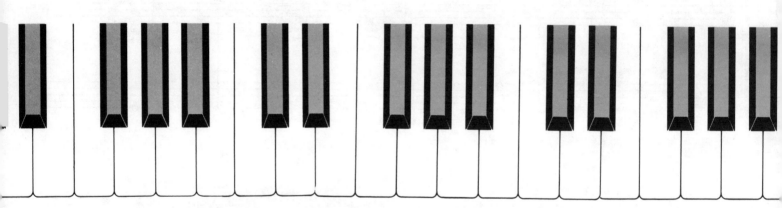

RECORDED ALBUMS BY THE AUTHOR

Outstanding Records
The Tatum Touch (solo)
Garmering The Blues (trio)
Cool Jazz (trio)
No One But Me (solo)
Touch of Elegance (solo)
Collection 1 (solo, duo & trio)
Collection 2 (solo, duo & trio)
Going for Baroque (piano & trpt.)
The Master Touch (duo)
The Ballad Touch (solo)
Paul Smith at Home (trio)

Fine Tune Records
Jazz on Broadway (trio)

Piano Disc
Artist Series (solo)